I0790262

This book belongs to

____

____

____

Alaric

the Vulpes Fulgen
first day at school

Written by Jamie Weston

Illustrated by Valentina P

Dear reader, this story contains some difficult words that have been purposely used to make the story fun to read and to help you grasp a wider vocabulary.

Words coloured in blue will feature an explanation in the glossary at the end. If you find other words difficult you are encouraged to seek help from a dictionary or adult.

If you would like to listen along to the **audiobook** version included in this book, please scan the QR code below.

Audiobook narrated by James Burton

Music by Emily Boddy

At the very base of the most ancient[1] oak, at the centre
of the deepest darkest wood, where archaic[2] trees tower
above the rest of the forest, whispering forgotten secrets
to the squirrels and the cuckoos, there resides a door too
small for any girl or boy to crawl through.

And if you're lucky enough to be visited by the old hag,
when she's done with feasting[3] on children, and if you're
sharp-witted enough to strike a fair deal, she may grant you
a tincture[4] to shrink you down to the size of a Pixie. For then
you would be able to venture through and discover a secret
realm beyond that enchanted[5] wooden door.

Beyond it, leads to another forest far, far away where the treetops sparkle like a cascade[6] of diamonds under the sun. They stretch high into the sky, their leaves a myriad[7] of silvered verdant[8] and aureate[9]. Some leaves even change colours, with the mood of the forest, creating a mesmerising[10] dance of hues with every gentle breeze. The canopy[11] above, so dense that it filters the sunlight into a soft, dappled glow, casting the forest floor in a perpetual[12] state of magical twilight, where everything seems to be bathed in a gentle, luminescent[13] glow.

The ground is carpeted with velvety moss so plush that with each step, one might feel as if they're walking on freshly sprung marshmallow. Interspersed[14] amongst the moss are flowers of every imaginable shape and colour. Some of these flowers hum soft lullabies, while others stand tall and firm like natural lamps, emitting a gentle moonlight hue, which illuminate the paths of travelling creatures that inhabit the forest.

Crystal-clear streams crisscross the forest, their waters gleaming with a sapphire[15] brilliance. The streams house fish that shimmer a mesmerising[16] dance, like a mermaid's tail while Bullytoads[17] with dark amber eyes and gem-encrusted skin, croak songs of forgotten tales.

And that's where, dear reader, our story begins, A tale of a quirky creature within this forest, named Alaric.

Imagine, if you will, a creature that resembled a type of red panda and a fennec fox hybrid[18]. Alaric sported fur that seemed like it was painted by a youngling, let loose with fiery red and soft cream crayons and with ears so large and pointed that he often joked they could pick up the local goblin radio stations. But when he wasn't busy tuning into pop songs with his ears, Alaric had hobbies that would make any young human nod in approval.

For he had an impressive collection of shiny pebbles, which he insisted were dragon treasures, he loved splashing in puddles during the monsoon[19] season and was a professional at building treehouses. (only to forget where he had built them, by the next morning.)

In short, Alaric was a delightful blend of mischief, wonder, and charm.

 This is a great place to take a break and continue the story next time.

At the far edge of the forest, nestled between the roots of a Giant Sequoia[20] which is a type of humongous[21] redwood tree, was Alaric's hide. His abode[22] was a blend of nature and comfort. The entrance was a round wooden door, adorned[23] with intricate[24] carvings of forest scenes, and fitted with a brass knob right in the centre.

Inside, the walls were lined with shelves carved directly into the earth, holding an array[25] of trinkets[26], books, and jars filled with mysterious ingredients. The floor was covered in plush rugs made from the softest feather moss, and in the centre of the living area stood a little wooden table, always ready for guests with a pot of tea and some freshly baked bug tarts.

In the centre, a small fireplace crackled away, its warm light dancing across the room and casting shadows that played hide and seek. Above the fireplace, a mantle showcased Alaric's most treasured possessions: a crystal his father had found in the mountain caves on his final expedition[27], a feather from a phoenix[28], and a photo of him with his momma.

The cosy burrow was always filled with the soft glow of the forest's twilight, filtering through the gaps in the roots above, making it a haven of warmth and safety for them both.

Alaric's morning began with the chirping of skylarks[29] and the distant sound of a stream. He would stretch his limbs, feeling the soft fur on his belly and the cool breeze from the window. With a yawn, he'd roll out of his snug bed, made of Nuzzlebear[30] fur and leaves, and begin his morning routine.

First, he'd pick up his tiny bamboo toothbrush, dab it with a bit of berry paste, and brush his teeth. He'd look at his reflection in a small puddle of water inside his hide, ensuring every tooth sparkled.

Next, he'd hop into his little tub, carved out of a hollowed log. He'd grab his bar of soap and after lathering[31] himself up, splash water over himself, scrubbing away the sleepiness with his paws. Once he was all clean, he'd shake himself dry, sending droplets flying in all directions.

Alaric then moved to his wardrobe, a nook in the wall filled with neatly folded clothes. He chose a soft tunic[32] made of woven grass and a pair of trousers that fit snugly around his waist. Slipping into them, he'd feel ready to face the day.

Before leaving his hide, Alaric would make his bed, tucking in the corners of his fur blanket and fluffing up his leafy pillow. He took pride in keeping his space tidy and helping his momma keep the hide clean. Emerging into the dining room, the aroma of bug porridge wafted through the air. His momma, with her gentle eyes and warm smile, would have a big bowl waiting for him.

"Eat up," she'd say, "You're a growing boy!" Alaric would devour the porridge, savouring every crunchy bug and sweet berry. A perfect filling breakfast for his first day at school. But he couldn't linger for long. As the sound of the worker ants marching towards the hide, signalled the arrival of the school bus.

Alaric took a deep breath and rushed out, his backpack bouncing, to find the massive log carried by the diligent ants with carved-out slots in the log holding seats for a plethora[33] of woodland creatures, with each slot tailored to the unique shapes and sizes of the forest's inhabitants.

 This is a great place to take a break and continue the story next time.

Alaric, with a mix of excitement and nervousness, searched for his designated spot and soon found himself nestled[34] between Alf, an Eldarish Leaf Squirrel[35], and a young Great Horned Snagtail[36] named Garret.

Alf was a fascinating creature. His body was covered in leaf-like flaps, resembling layers of cabbage. These flaps served as a natural camouflage[37], allowing him to blend seamlessly into the trees. The forest elves often chose the Eldarish Leaf Squirrels as their companions due to their shared love for the treetops and their ability to move silently among the branches.

Beside Alf was the Great Horned Snagtail, a creature that looked like a horned snail the size of a rabbit. With its majestic horns and a long, iridescent[38] tail, the Snagtail was a sight to behold. Its exoskeleton[39] shimmered in the dappled sunlight filtering through the trees, and its large, expressive eyes held a hint of mischief. Snagtails, though mostly harmless, are known to be the best friends of the Goblins for their cunning and bouts of rascality[40].

As the log bus trundled along, the Snagtail leaned closer
to Alaric and Alf, his voice barely above a whisper. "I heard
that at school, the older boys and girls grab you by the
tail, flush your head into the toilet, and eat your lunch," he
murmured, his eyes wide with a mix of fear and intrigue.

Alf's leafy flaps rustled, a sign of his discomfort. "That's just
a silly rumour," he replied, trying to sound confident. "But
we should stick together, just in case." Garrick the Snagtail
turned back facing away from them both, a wicked smile
emerging across its slimy face.

Alaric nodded in agreement, feeling a bond forming
between the three of them. The journey to school, filled
with whispered tales and shared anxieties[41], was the
beginning of a friendship that would see them through
many adventures.

Being the first day of school, Alaric felt the vastness of the great forest clearing envelop[42] him. The school wasn't like any ordinary building; it was a series of ancient halfling mounds, long abandoned by their original inhabitants and now repurposed for the education of the forest's young creatures.

These mounds, made of wood, mud, and lichen[43], stood tall and proud, their surfaces intricately carved with beautiful ornate designs. Each carving told tales of their ancestors, and in the centre of the main mound was a grand depiction of Sunra, the God of peace and happiness, with rays of sunlight emanating[44] from its figure.

As Alaric stood tepidly[45] in the bustling courtyard, he observed the other new students. Creatures of all shapes and sizes chattered and chirped excitedly, their voices blending into a harmonious cacophony[46] that echoed through the clearing. But amidst the excitement, Alaric felt like a tiny acorn lost in a vast forest. He felt out of place, an anomaly[47] in this new vibrant world.

 This is a great place to take a break and continue the story next time.

His eyes darted around, searching for something familiar or comforting. That's when he noticed the painted lines on the ground, guiding students towards various playground games. There was hopscotch, a maze, and even a spiral pattern that seemed to lead to the centre of the courtyard used for games of Puffball.

With nervous energy bubbling within him, Alaric decided to occupy his time with the lines. He traced them with his paw, following their winding paths. But as he moved further, he noticed sections where the paint had faded, eroded[48] by time and countless footsteps.

An idea sparked in his mind. Finding a chunk of broken shale on the floor and with meticulous[49] care, he began to fill in the eroded lines, trying to restore them to their former glory. He became so engrossed in his task that he lost track of time.

Suddenly, the school bell's chime echoed through the clearing, signaling the start of classes. The creatures of the wood hurried towards the school's grand entrance, ready for another year of learning but as Alaric looked up, he found himself face to face with a tall, imposing teacher.

Her eyes, sharp and stern, bore into him. "Young one," she said with a hint of reprimand[50], "this is not how we treat our sacred grounds on the first day or any day."

Embarrassed, Alaric was handed a dustpan and brush. He cleaned up his freshly laid marks, his cheeks burning with shame. Once he finished, he hurriedly made his way to his first class late, hoping the rest of the day would be kinder to him.

As he entered his first class, he saw all of the other students sitting at their desks with pencils in hand and books open ready to take notes, Alaric spotted an empty chair right at the back, his head tipped low as he shyly manoeuvred[51] through rows of strangers, but as he sat down and opened his bag, a wave of panic suddenly washed over Alaric. He realised he had forgotten his pencil.

The teacher, a stern Strix[52], a creature similar to a Scops Owl with piercing eyes, fixed her gaze on him. "You must always come prepared," she hooted in a tone that left no room for excuses.

Alaric's large ears drooped in embarrassment, making him feel even smaller in the vast classroom. From a few desks away, Garrick the Snagtail couldn't contain his amusement and sniggered, his little snorts echoing throughout the mound, amplifying Alaric's discomfort. However, Alf, ever the kind-hearted squirrel, leaned over and whispered, "Don't worry, I have a spare pencil you can borrow. Just remember to bring yours tomorrow."

Alaric gave a grateful smile, replying, "Thanks, Alf. I'm just trying to get the hang of all this."

 This is a great place to take a break and continue the story next time.

During lunchtime, Alaric found himself following a queue that led towards a grand hall. The tantalising[53] aroma[54] of various dishes wafted through the air, mingling with the steam that rose from large cauldrons[55] and pots.

The hall buzzed with activity, as teachers and pupils of all ages and sizes came together in a communal feast. The walls echoed with laughter, chatter, and the clinking of cutlery.

As Alaric approached the front of the queue, a lunch assistant, a spritely pixie with a clipboard, fluttered up to him. "Dinners or packed lunch?" she inquired, her voice melodic yet brisk. Alaric blinked in confusion, "What?" The pixie pointed to a sign overhead. On it, two symbols were depicted: one for a packed lunch pointing left and another for school dinners pointing right.

After a moment of hesitation[56], Alaric remembered the handful of coins his momma had given him that morning. "Dinner, please!" he replied, his voice tinged with relief. "Very well, young pup. Follow this line," the pixie instructed, pointing him towards the right.

With his tray laden with a variety of dishes including carrot puree[57], roach bread and pepperstem soup, Alaric began his search for a place to sit. He was met with a series of confusing signs and unspoken rules.

A centaur[58], munching on a salad, pointed to a sign that read, "Quadrupeds[59] Only." Another time, he approached a dimly lit table, only to be shooed away by a group of goblins who informed him it was reserved for "Underground Dwellers", He turned another corner and sat down to suddenly hear a small voice "This is for herbivores only," a River Slug said, pointing to a sign. Another time, he was shooed away from a table for nocturnal animals. The labyrinthine[60] rules of the school seemed impossible to navigate.

Feeling lost in the maze of the dining hall, Alaric's ears perked up when he heard a familiar voice. "Over here, Alaric!" called Alf, waving him over to a table where their classroom friends sat.

Gratefully, Alaric made his way over and was introduced to Grizelda, a yellow-crested chickenmouse with feathery wings and a gentle demeanour and a storm golem[61] called Bo. The group welcomed him warmly, and amidst the shared stories and laughter, Alaric felt a sense of belonging.

 This is a great place to take a break and continue the story next time.

In the afternoon, still trying to navigate the maze-like corridors of the school, Alaric mistakenly wandered into a room that was bathed in a soft, golden light. The walls of the room were adorned with intricate mosaics[62] depicting mythical creatures dancing under a canopy of stars. The floor was polished to a mirror sheen, reflecting the delicate twig and horn chandeliers[63] that hung from the ceiling, each one twinkling with a myriad of tiny, enchanted baubles[64].

To his astonishment, Alaric found himself amidst a dance class. The room was filled with ethereal[65] Lunamaidens[66] and Sunsprites[67]. The Lunamaidens, with their luminescent skin and flowing silver gowns, moved with grace that mimicked the gentle pull of the tides. The Sunsprites, on the other hand, were radiant beings that seemed to shimmer with an inner light, their dance steps lively and vibrant, reminiscent of the sun's rays piercing through morning mist.

As the music swelled, a delicate melody played by unseen musicians, Alaric felt a rising panic. He believed he would be asked to join this mesmerising dance. With his clumsy fuzzy paws, he felt out of place amidst such grace and beauty. And as he tried to back away discreetly, he stumbled over his own feet, causing a minor disruption in the dance.

The room filled with soft, tinkling laughter. A Lunamaiden, her eyes kind but amused, floated over to him. "Lost, are we?" she asked with a gentle smile. Flustered, Alaric nodded, his large ears drooping in embarrassment. "I thought this was maths class," he mumbled. The Sunsprite next to the Lunamaiden chuckled, "Well, you're a few corridors away, but don't worry. We all get lost sometimes."

With their guidance, Alaric soon found his way to the
maths department, but the memory of the enchanting
dance room and its gracious inhabitants stayed with
him for a long time. He entered the first room on his left.
The room was a mathematician's dream. From floor to
ceiling, chalkboards covered the walls, filled with complex
equations[68], graphs, and diagrams.

Tables were laden with intriguing mathematical
equipment: golden compasses with intricate designs,
protractors[69] made of shimmering crystal, and strange
measuring instruments that seemed to move and adjust
on their own. The air was thick with the scent of chalk and
the quiet hum of concentration.

The lesson for the day was on particularly advanced
mathematical topics. To Alaric, it sounded like a foreign
language. Words like "algebraic equations[70]," and "geometry
patterns[71]", floated around the room, making his head spin.
He tried to jot down notes, but his book was filled with
scribbles and symbols that made little sense to him.

As he was trying to decipher[72] his own handwriting, the teacher, a wise old tortoise with spectacles perched on his snout, turned to him and asked, "Can you tell us the solution to this equation?"

The world seemed to shrink around Alaric. The walls of the classroom closed in, and a suffocating darkness enveloped him. Beads of sweat formed on his furry brow, and his heart raced. In a desperate attempt to answer, he blurted out the first number that came to mind, "Um... 42?"

The room went silent. The teacher paused, adjusting his spectacles and studying Alaric for a moment. Then, in a calm and gentle voice, he said, "An answer more suited to our philosophy[73] lectures I think, you seem a little young to be attending advanced mathematics, I think you will have a less stressful time next door" the tortoise directed him to a sign that said 'Year 1 maths'.

 This is a great place to take a break and continue the story next time.

MATH 101

Alaric sighed in relief, grateful for the teacher's understanding. The weight on his chest lifted slightly, and he made a mental note to always seek help when lost.

After the whirlwind of numbers and equations in maths class, Alaric was relieved to see that his next class was art. The art room in the school was a place of wonder. The walls were adorned with paintings and drawings of magical creatures, enchanted forests, and starry night skies. Tables were scattered with an array of art supplies: brushes of all sizes, palettes filled with vibrant colours, and pots of glittering red and silver dust.

As Alaric entered, he felt a wave of nostalgia[74]. Back in his hide, he often doodled and painted, capturing the beauty of the forest and its inhabitants. He felt a sense of confidence, thinking that this was one class where he could truly shine.

The teacher, Miss. Selene, a graceful Moonmoth[75] with iridescent wings, fluttered to the front of the class. "Today," she began with a soft, melodic voice, "we will be exploring the art of paper mache. We'll be creating sculptures of our favourite magical creatures."

The class buzzed with excitement. Alaric's mind raced with ideas. Should he create a miniature version of a Great Horned Snagtail? Or perhaps a delicate Eldarish Leaf Squirrel?

He decided on crafting a model of his own home, the ancient Redwood tree, complete with its intricate roots and the cosy hide nestled within. He began with enthusiasm, tearing strips of paper, dipping them into the gooey paste, and layering them onto his balloon base.

However, as he was engrossed in his work, he didn't notice that the pot of wet paper mache paste was precariously[76] close to the edge of the table. With an accidental nudge of his elbow, the pot tipped over, sending a cascade of gooey paste right onto Garrick, the Great Horned Snagtail.

Garrick sat there, stunned, covered from head to tail in the sticky mess. The paste dripped from his majestic horns, and his once shimmering fur now clumped together in wet patches. The room went silent for a heartbeat, and then erupted in a mixture of gasps and giggles.

Alaric's ears drooped, and his cheeks turned a shade redder than his fur. "I'm so sorry, Garrick!" he exclaimed, rushing over with a cloth, trying to help clean up the mess.

Garrick, although surprised, managed a chuckle. "Well, I did say I wanted to become a work of art one day," he joked, trying to lighten the mood.

Miss Selene fluttered over, her wings creating a soft breeze. "Accidents happen," she said gently. "But let's make sure we're more careful next time."

The rest of the lesson went by in a blur of laughter, creativity, and a few more minor mishaps. By the end, the room was filled with an array of colourful, albeit slightly lopsided, magical creatures.

As the bell rang, signalling the end of the class, Alaric approached Garrick, "I'm really sorry about earlier," he said sincerely.

Garrick smiled, "It's alright. Just remember, next time you want to make a masterpiece, try not to use me as the canvas!"

As the end of the day drew near, Alaric felt defeated. The vastness of the school, the unspoken rules, and the constant feeling of being out of place weighed on him.

He felt trapped in a world that didn't understand him,
the distant sound of the bell echoed through the
school, signalling the end of the day. Alaric gathered his
belongings and, with the day's adventures replaying in his
mind, made his way to the school bus.

However, as he was about to leave, a soft, comforting voice
reached out to him. It was Grizelda, "The first day is always
a little tricky," she whispered, her voice as soothing as a
distant star's twinkle. "But remember, every new friend was
once a stranger, and every expert was once a beginner.
You'll find your way, just like the rest of us did."

Alaric gazed into her kind, understanding eyes, and felt a
warmth spread through him, like a cosy blanket on a chilly
night. He realised that in this vast, magical world, there
was a special nook just waiting for him to discover.

The familiar log carried by the diligent ants awaited him, and as he climbed aboard, he found his seat next to Alf and the others.

The journey back through the forest was filled with the soft chatter of his newfound friends, recounting the day's events and sharing their own tales. With each passing moment, Alaric felt a growing sense of belonging. As the bus trundled along, the weight of the morning's anxieties began to lift, replaced by a budding optimism.[77]

By the time he reached his cosy hide, nestled between the roots of the ancient tree, Alaric felt a renewed sense of hope. With the warmth of his home welcoming him and the promise of another day ahead, he went to bed feeling positive and eager for the adventures the next day would bring.

GLOSSARY

- 1 Ancient
  - Meaning: Very old; from a long time ago.
  - Pronunciation: AYN-shent
- 2 Archaic
  - Meaning: Very old and not used now.
  - Pronunciation: ar-KAY-ik
- 3 Feasting
  - Meaning: Eating a big meal, often for a celebration.
  - Pronunciation: FEES-ting
- 4 Tincture
  - Meaning: A medicine made by mixing a drug in alcohol; a tiny bit of something.
  - Pronunciation: TINK-chur
- 5 Enchanted
  - Meaning: Filled with wonder or magic.
  - Pronunciation: en-CHAN-ted
- 6 Cascade
  - Meaning: A small waterfall.
  - Pronunciation: kuh-SKAYD
- 7 Myriad
  - Meaning: A countless or extremely great number of people or things; innumerable; existing in large numbers.
  - Pronunciation: Meer-ee-ad

- **8 Verdant**
  - Meaning: Green with plants or grass.
  - Pronunciation: VER-dant

- **9 Aureate**
  - Meaning: Golden or shiny.
  - Pronunciation: OR-ee-at

- **10 Mesmerising**
  - Meaning: So interesting or beautiful that it grabs your attention.
  - Pronunciation: MEZ-muh-rye-zing

- **11 Canopy**
  - Meaning: A cover or shade, like the top part of a forest or a cloth over a bed.
  - Pronunciation: CAN-uh-pee

- **12 Perpetual**
  - Meaning: Never ending or always happening.
  - Pronunciation: per-PET-chu-ul

- **13 Luminescent**
  - Meaning: Giving off light without heat.
  - Pronunciation: loo-muh-NESS-ent

- **14 Interspersed**
  - Meaning: Scattered among or between other things.
  - Pronunciation: in-ter-SPURST

- **15 Sapphire**
  - Meaning: A precious blue gemstone.
  - Pronunciation: SAF-fyer

- **16 Mesmerising**
  - Meaning: So interesting or beautiful that it grabs your attention.
  - Pronunciation: MEZ-muh-rye-zing
- **17 Bullytoads**
  - Meaning: A Fantasy reptile that is similar to a large grumpy frog encrusted with gems created by the author inspired by the Cane / Bull Toad.
  - Pronunciation: BULL-EE-Towed

- **18 Hybrid**
  - Meaning: A thing made by combining two different elements.
  - Pronunciation: HIGH-brid
- **19 Monsoon**
  - Meaning: A seasonal wind, often bringing heavy rain.
  - Pronunciation: mon-SOON
- **20 Giant Sequoia**
  - Meaning: A very large tree native to California, Also known as a Giant RedWood.
  - Pronunciation: JYE-ant seh-KWOY-uh
- **21 Humongous**
  - Meaning: Extremely large; enormous.
  - Pronunciation: Huh-mun-gus
- **22 Abode**
  - Meaning: A place of residence; a house or home.
  - Pronunciation: Uh-bohd

- **23 Adorned**
  - Meaning: Decorated or made more attractive with ornaments or other decorative items.
  - Pronunciation: Uh-dawrnd
- **24 Intricate**
  - Meaning: Very detailed or complicated in design or structure.
  - Pronunciation: In-tri-kit
- **25 Array**
  - Meaning: An ordered series or arrangement of things or a collection of items, especially one that is impressive or large.
  - Pronunciation: Uh-ray
- **26 Trinkets**
  - Meaning: Small ornaments or items, often of little value but cherished for other reasons, such as their sentimental value or decorative nature.
  - Pronunciation: Trin-kits
- **27 Expedition**
  - Meaning: A journey for a specific purpose, like exploring.
  - Pronunciation: ex-peh-DISH-un
- **28 Phoenix**
  - Meaning: A mythical bird that is reborn from its ashes.
  - Pronunciation: FEE-niks

- **29 Skylarks**
  - Meaning: Small brown birds known for their song while flying.
  - Pronunciation: SKYE-larks

- **30 Nuzzlebear**
  - Meaning: A fantasy creature created by the author, seemingly sweet and endearing creature resembling a teddy bear during the day. However, by night, it undergoes a startling transformation, growing gigantic spider-like fangs and becoming a nocturnal hunter.
  - Pronunciation: Nuh-zul-bare

- **31 Lathering**
  - Meaning: Covering with a thick layer of soap bubbles.
  - Pronunciation: LATH-er-ing

- **32 Tunic**
  - Meaning: A loose garment, typically sleeveless.
  - Pronunciation: TOO-nik

- **33 Plethora**
  - Meaning: A large amount of something.
  - Pronunciation: PLETH-uh-ruh

- **34 Nestled**
  - Meaning: Settled snugly or comfortably.
  - Pronunciation: NES-uld

- **35 Eldarish Leaf Squirrel**

  - Meaning: A fictional squirrel species created by the author known for its unique appearance. Its body is covered in leaf-like flaps that resemble layers of cabbage.
  - Pronunciation: EL-dah-rish LEAF SKWURR-el

- **36 Great Horned Snagtail**
  - Meaning: A fictional creature created by the author that appears to be a combination of a horned snail the size of rabbit. With its majestic horns and a long, elegant tail that looks like the rainbows you see in oil. Its soft fur shimmers in the sunlight, and its large, expressive eyes hold a hint of mischief.
  - Pronunciation: Grayt HORND SNAG-tayl

- **37 Camouflage**
  - Meaning: A way of hiding something (often by making it look like its surroundings).
  - Pronunciation: CAM-oh-flahj

- **38 Iridescent**
  - Meaning: Showing many bright colours that change with movement.
  - Pronunciation: ear-ih-DESS-ent

- **39 Exoskeleton**
  - Meaning: A rigid external covering for the body in some invertebrate animals, especially arthropods (like insects, spiders, and crustaceans), providing both support and protection.
  - Pronunciation: EK-soh-SKEL-uh-tuhn

- **40 Rascality**
  - Meaning: Mischievous behaviour.
  - Pronunciation: ras-KAL-ih-tee

- **41 Anxieties**
  - Meaning: Feelings of worry or nervousness.
  - Pronunciation: ang-ZYE-uh-tees

- 42 Envelop
  - Meaning: To wrap up or cover completely.
  - Pronunciation: en-VELL-up

- 43 Lichen
  - Meaning: A simple plant that grows on rocks, walls, and trees.
  - Pronunciation: LY-ken

- 44 Emanating
  - Meaning: To come out from a source; to emit or send forth.
  - Pronunciation: Em-uh-nay-ting

- 45 Tepidly
  - Meaning: In a lukewarm or half-hearted manner; without enthusiasm or energy.
  - Pronunciation: Teh-pid-lee

- 46 Cacophony
  - Meaning: A harsh, discordant mixture of sounds.
  - Pronunciation: Kuh-koff-uh-nee

- 47 Anomaly
  - Meaning: Something that deviates from what is standard, normal, or expected.
  - Pronunciation: Uh-nom-uh-lee

- 48 Eroded
  - Meaning: Worn away gradually, usually by water or wind.
  - Pronunciation: ih-ROH-ded

- 49 Meticulous
  - Meaning: Very careful and with great attention to detail.
  - Pronunciation: meh-TIK-yoo-lus

- **50 Reprimand**
  - Meaning: A formal expression of disapproval or criticism.
  - Pronunciation: Rep-ri-mand

- **51 Manoeuvred**
  - Meaning: Moved skillfully or carefully.
  - Pronunciation: muh-NOO-verd

- **52 Strix**
  - Meaning: A type of owl from mythology of classical books that was a bird of ill omen, that fed on human flesh and blood. It also referred to witches and related malevolent folkloric beings.
  - Pronunciation: Str-icks

- **53 Tantalising**
  - Meaning: Teasing or tempting by remaining just out of reach.
  - Pronunciation: TAN-tuh-lye-zing

- **54 Aroma**
  - Meaning: A pleasant and distinctive smell.
  - Pronunciation: uh-ROH-muh

- **55 Cauldrons**
  - Meaning: Large metal pots with a handle and lid, used for cooking over an open fire.
  - Pronunciation: KAWL-drinz

- **56 Hesitation**
  - Meaning: A pause or delay in acting or deciding.
  - Pronunciation: hez-ih-TAY-shun

- 57 Puree
  - Meaning: A smooth, creamy substance made of liquidised or crushed fruit or vegetables.
  - Pronunciation: pyoo-RAY
- 58 Centaur
  - Meaning: A mythical creature with the upper body of a human and the lower body of a horse.
  - Pronunciation: SEN-tawr
- 59 Quadrupeds
  - Meaning: Animals that walk on four legs.
  - Pronunciation: KWOD-roo-peds

- 60 Labyrinthine
  - Meaning: Relating to or resembling a labyrinth; very complicated or intricate.
  - Pronunciation: lab-uh-RIN-thine
- 61 Golem
  - Meaning: A mythical creature made of clay or mud that's brought to life.
  - Pronunciation: GOH-lem
- 62 Mosaics
  - Meaning: Pictures or patterns made by placing small coloured pieces of hard material together.
  - Pronunciation: moh-ZAY-iks
- 63 Chandeliers
  - Meaning: Decorative hanging lights with branches for several light bulbs or candles.
  - Pronunciation: shan-duh-LEERS

- **64 Baubles**
  - Meaning: Small, shiny ornaments or trinkets.
  - Pronunciation: BAW-buls
- **65 Ethereal**
  - Meaning: Extremely delicate and light in a way that seems not of this world.
  - Pronunciation: eh-THEER-ee-ul
- **66 Lunamaidens**
  - Meaning: Mythical or fantasy beings often associated with the moon. They are typically depicted as ethereal and luminescent creatures, embodying the gentle and calming qualities of the moon. Created by the author.
  - Pronunciation: Loona-may-denz
- **67 Sunsprites**
  - Meaning: Mythical or fantasy beings often associated with the sun. They are usually imagined as radiant and glowing creatures, representing the vibrant and energetic qualities of the sun. Created by the author.
  - Pronunciation: SUN-spryts
- **68 Equations**
  - Meaning: Mathematical statements that two things are equal.
  - Pronunciation: ih-KWAY-zhuns
- **69 Protractors**
  - Meaning: A tool used in geometry to measure and draw angles. It's typically a semi-circular shape with degree markings.
  - Pronunciation: proh-TRAK-torz

- **70 Algebraic Equations**
  - Meaning: Mathematical statements that show the relationship between two expressions separated by an equal sign (=). They contain one or more variables (like x or y) that represent unknown values.
  - Pronunciation: al-juh-BRAY-ik ee-KWAY-zhuns
- **71 Geometry Patterns**
  - Meaning: Patterns or sequences found within shapes and lines in geometry. These can include repeating shapes, symmetrical designs, or sequences of angles.
  - Pronunciation: jee-AH-muh-tree PAT-urns
- **72 Decipher**
  - Meaning: To figure out or interpret.
  - Pronunciation: dih-SY-fur
- **73 Philosophy**
  - Meaning: The study of fundamental questions about existence, knowledge, and ethics.
  - Pronunciation: fuh-LOSS-uh-fee
- **74 Nostalgia**
  - Meaning: A sentimental longing for the past.
  - Pronunciation: nah-STAL-juh
- **75 Moonmoth**
  - Meaning: A fictional or mythical humanoid moth created by the author that is often associated with the moon, typically imagined as having a soft glow or being active during the night. In real life exists a luna moth *(Actias luna)*, which is also called the American moon moth but this is not related.
  - Pronunciation: MOON-mawth

- **76 Precariously**
  - Meaning: In a way that is not securely in position and is likely to fall.
  - Pronunciation: prih-KAIR-ee-us-lee
- **77 Optimism**
  - Meaning: Hopefulness and confidence about the future.
  - Pronunciation: OP-tuh-miz-um
- **Vulpes Fulgen**
  - A Fantasy mammal that is half Fennec Fox and Half Red Panda created by the author using a mixture of the animals latin names (Vulpes zerda - Fennec fox and Ailurus fulgens - Red Panda).